FADING DARKNESS

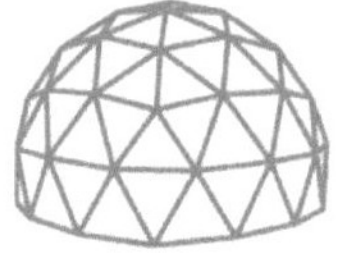

TURN ON THE LIGHT
WITHIN YOU

Sebastian Schick

Edited by Cheryl Chen

**Fading Darkness:
Turn On the Light Within You
ISBN: 9783741204814**

Copyright © Sebastian Schick 2016
Cover Design © Eduardo Enrique Meza 2016
Text edited by Cheryl Chen

First published in Germany in 2016 by Books on
Demand (Germany).

Books on Demand
Gutenbergring 53
22848 Norderstedt
Germany
www.bod.de

This book is a work of fiction and, except in the case of
historical fact, any resemblance to actual persons,
living or dead, is purely coincidental.

Ordering Information:
Print version available for order on www.amazon.com
and www.barnesandnoble.com.
E-book version available for order on Kindle, Google
Play and iBookstore.
For bulk order details, or orders by trade bookstores
and wholesalers, please contact Books on Demand
(Germany) at the address above, at tel: +49 40-53 43
35-11 or visit www.bod.de.

For invitations to speaking or book events, contact the
author at www.sebastianschick.com.

Printed and bound in Germany by Books on Demand.

For Tze Lin…

It was love at first sight and I have no doubt that it is by God's grace that I met you. The one person without whom this book would never have been written.

You are, and always will be, The One.

Tze Lin, I love you.

Acknowledgments

My greatest support in life has always been my family, friends and especially my parents. Leonhard and Claudia Schick. I know that everything that I am today, and all the things that I am doing, are based on your love and the values that you have planted in me.

Thank you so much.

They say that there is a book inside all of us. If that's true, very few of us ever let it out. We keep it buried in the dark along with many of our fears, hopes and dreams. Perhaps, for most of us, where we keep our book is a magical place that we only visit on our own.

Sometimes however, a young person has the courage to look into that place and share it with the world. Sometimes we get a glimpse of what this magical place looks like for someone else and in so doing are able to reflect on our own lives.

Sebastian beautifully shares Encora with us and in so doing we not only get to know him better, but also ourselves.

Mark Hemstedt
Founding Partner
The Works Partnership

Foreword: A Compelling Future.

This book is a beautiful combination of the ideal future and childhood fantasy. Both ingredients, when mixed, makes for nostalgia, inspiration and hope that every reader can design a future that is compelling.

Sebastian writes with warmth, tenderness and sincerity and invites the reader to come into his world and play. He also writes with universal themes - dreaming, relationships, choice, love, beauty, obstacles, belief, death, with summaries at the end that bring further relevance of the text to life.

Kudos to Sebastian for transforming his vision and passion into words that will no doubt inspire many readers worldwide.

Here's to life!

Tini Fadzillah
Founding Partner
The Works Partnership

Foreword: A Great Dream.

I've known Sebastian for a long time and I've really enjoyed reading his first book.

Sebastian is a man with a great dream, and like all men with great dreams, he is growing day by day while in pursuit of that dream. In his thoughts, words and deeds, Sebastian constantly seeks to create a world of opportunities for anyone and everyone, regardless of who they are and where they come from. With this book, he is not just making a dream come true; he's leading a life of intention and purpose, and I am incredibly proud of him.

Reading this book supported me in creating self-awareness and reflecting on my own experiences. I could easily identify with the story of the city of Encora and the main character. The writing style is simple, clear and relatable, which made it easy for me to follow the storyline and go in-depth with the insights at the end of each chapter.

This book will help you to rethink your situations and experiences and encourage you to take further steps towards powerful change in your life, towards a life of making a difference.

Thank you, Sebastian, for this wonderful, inspirational and motivational book. I hope that many other people are as inspired by your book as I am.

Titus Lindl
Founder of WEGVISOR© and Founding Partner at The John Maxwell Team

Contents

Introduction

What could I start a story with, which hasn't yet been told? This moment in which I'm writing, the story hasn't ended yet. It has only just begun. Not that I haven't imagined what I wish would be the end of the story; I have. I wish it would be something like "and they kissed each other like the sun touching the sea when it sets, and he whispered softly, 'I love you forever.'" Yes, it's really cheesy, but that's me. So, as you can see, I did imagine how the end could look like.

The thing is, this isn't just some random story. This is a story about the light within you. If you have ever wanted to see a breakthrough, you are about to witness it. This book could be the blueprint for your life. I'm going to show you something you have never seen before, something that may awaken the brave hero inside of you. The part of you which isn't bound by the limitations of your mind. And the most beautiful thing about it is, it's all true. If the reality of your capability becomes accessible to you, like when you become aware of the fact that you are more powerful then you can see right now, you will finally be free.

Throughout the time that you read this book, I want you to open up your heart to one question and one question only: What would your life look like if you honestly believed that you are enough and that your life matters? Because it does!

Sebastian Schick
Author

How to Read this Story

There is no particular way to read this book. There may be moments that inspire much thought, or bring to mind many parallels with your own life. You may gain some insights along the way. Perhaps you may even experience some emotions. When this happens, I encourage you to find a pen and start writing. I've included note pages after every chapter for you to pen your thoughts down.

Many of us have very good thoughts, but only a few really think about a good thought. You all know the saying: "experience is the greatest teacher". But actually, that is not completely true. This is more accurate: "reflection on each experience is the greatest teacher". Reflection and a long thinking process help us to extract wisdom out of our own experiences and the experiences of others.

That is why I invite you, whenever a thought, feeling or memory comes up while you're reading this book, to pause and give it some space. Experience it. It might be wisdom coming after you.

So take the time you need to work through the book. Don't be shy. Make some notes in the note pages provided. Make it your own story and bring that deepest dream of yours to life by shining as the brightest light that you can be. I honestly believe you can.

Fading Darkness

Turn On the Light Within You

Chapter One: The Dream

"Good morning Mr Braunsten." I had come to school earlier to make sure I got a chance to see the principal to talk about a crazy wish of mine. "Mr Braunsten, I would like to change my free elective subject". That meant I would have to repeat my final year. According to the rules, every student had to choose a free elective subject to study for one whole year. The free elective class was meant to prepare students for their future career, and if they changed their mind later, they needed to do over the whole year! No exception was ever given.

I had had a crazy dream one week ago, a dream in which I saw Encora, the city I live in, before it became what it is now – the last remaining city in the world. It was beautiful walking along the streets of the past, seeing the people of old who shaped our city. When I woke up, I couldn't get rid of the feeling that I had to change my free elective.

"Mr Braunsten. I would like to choose another free elective," I said, looking straight at him. Mr Braunsten looked like any other teacher, yet there was something subtly different about him. His brown beard was neatly trimmed and his hair was long enough to be combed to the back. The distinct wrinkles next to his eyes revealed his age and spoke much about his life. This was a man who had witnessed many things beyond these walls, which, in our generation, made him the best person to teach and prepare us for a future in this world, where there's so much fear and uncertainty.

"You know that this means you will have to do your final year again, right?" He replied, looking at me with mild confusion and interest, all the while examining my face to see if my gaze wavered. It didn't.

"Yes I do, Mr Braunsten. But I really want to take another free elective instead. I've realized that I never wanted to do Guard Training in the first place. I was just too afraid to do what my heart told me to do. I didn't want anyone to laugh at me, so I chose the same thing that all the other boys chose," I explained, voice trembling.

Curiosity piqued, he asked, "And what is your heart telling you to do?"

"Hero History," I answered, and showed him a letter from my grandpa. He took it and read through it carefully.

I didn't know what my grandpa had written in the letter. When I told my grandpa about my dream and the impact it had on me, he said, "Follow your heart and it will lead you well". My heart was pounding as I thought he would object to me delaying my graduation and my service to Encora. But he had merely looked at me, a twinkle in his eye, and told me to fetch him a pen and some paper. Then he had sat at the kitchen table for an hour, carefully penning the letter that was now in Mr Braunsten's hands. And now, as Mr Braunsten's eyes swept through the lines of the letter, they started to twinkle as well.

"Yes... the ability lies in us, it always has. Love will be the birth of justice, indeed," Mr Braunsten muttered, as grandpa spoke to him from the pages of the letter. I frowned, puzzled; that line sounded familiar. Was Mr Braunsten talking to me? Before I could ask, Mr Braunsten took a deep breath and the subtle smile he tried to hide behind his beard now disappeared.

"I'm going to be straightforward with you," he said softly, looking up at me. "Never before have I been in such a situation. There is an opportunity to re-do the final year but no one has ever done it." He paused for a few seconds, deep in thought. I kept quiet, fingers crossed, not daring to interrupt his thoughts for fear that he would say no. Then he smiled once more at the letter in his hands and said, "I will grant your request." He signed the letter and gave it back to me with a note for my new teacher. I felt my heart flutter with excitement as I stood up to go. Before I left Mr Braunsten's office, he said, "I think it is a good choice."

"Thank you, Mr Braunsten."

This was the first thing I had wanted to do this morning, and I'd done it. I was so relieved. Though I didn't know how everything would be from now on, I did it anyway. That was all that mattered. It felt like I had finally embarked on my destiny.

My school was located right in the heart of Encora. In the morning, the school bus would pass through our street and stop in front of my great-grandfather's house. Walking down our front yard each day, I would look around my neighborhood, each time trying to spot something I hadn't noticed the day before. Like the missing brick on top of the Peterson's chimney across the street. Or the white cat sitting on the front porch rail of our neighbours next door, the Schmitts – a German family who had lived there longer than I could remember. Although every single house on our street was unique, they all had red roofs that were neatly lined up like arrows pointing towards the city centre, and the school.

The Hero History class was on the other side of the vast school building. I walked across the immense courtyard, passed a giant sculpture of a young boy, and entered the building again. This was a section of the school I had never been to before. It was the oldest part of the school compound, with high beams and intricate paintings on almost every wall. I didn't have time to admire it, though. Room number 122, where my new class was, was at the end of the nearest corridor. The paintings lining the walls of the corridor blurred as I raced past, already late for class.

The door was closed, so I knocked. "Yes," I heard from inside the classroom. I opened the door and stepped in. All eyes were instantly on me – a frightening experience.

"Yes, what is it, please?" The teacher tried to get my attention. "How can I help?" he asked.

"Oh, excuse me. I'm a new student of yours I think." I handed him the note from Mr Braunsten.

"Okay. Well. Take a seat. Guys, it seems like we have a new classmate."

It felt like the looks from everyone in the class were passing right through me. They seemed to care as much about me as a leaf falling from a tree in autumn. I walked towards the back of the classroom, between the tables, carefully, so I wouldn't hit anyone with my bag. I passed a guy who was sketching dragons in his notebook, and made brief eye contact with another guy who was sitting next to an empty chair. His long, brown hair and his sneer caught my attention. Something in his eyes told me that this class was going to be tough. We acknowledged each other with a nod while I was sitting down right next to him. This moment felt so unreal.

Today's class was almost over when the teacher asked, "Who here still believes in the old prophecy?" Something inside me began to feel really warm. I couldn't ignore the feeling. And before I even knew what I was doing, I was already raising my hand. I knew it, I did.

Insights:
The free elective class represents the decision you took about what life you wanted to live. Sometimes we choose something that isn't really the dream we have in our heart of hearts. So the question for you to reflect on is: When and for what reason did you compromise your dream because of the world around you?

NOTES

14

Chapter Two: Prophecy & Poetry

The guy looked at me as if I had just insulted him.

"Did I understand you correctly? You believe in the prophecy?"

The way he said it, it wasn't just a question. His tone was ominous, even threatening. It was truly one of the most terrifying moments of my life. He was the guy in the leather jacket, always teasing everyone and perpetually surrounded by people who seemed to like everything he said, or were too afraid to disagree with him. Before today, I only knew him from the school bus. His face was the only one that looked familiar when I stepped into this new class just one hour ago.

"Yes, I do." I said, not knowing how I'd gotten myself into this situation. Usually no one recognised me. That was over the moment I'd raised my hand. I was the skinny guy with no friends, no interesting stories and nobody ever surrounded me. I was what you would call 'the other side of the coin'. The side that always landed in the dirt. I wasn't smart enough to not raise my hand. On the contrary, I was the only person who did. So there I was, every eyeball staring at me. For the next twenty minutes I was asking myself why I raised my hand. The situation didn't change even when the lesson was over. After the teacher had left, everyone stood up and approached the corner of the room where I was told to sit.

"Did I understand you correctly? You believe in the prophecy?"

"Yes, I do!"

Encora was once a wonderful place, inhabited by people that were full of passion and chivalry. The people of Encora used to believe so strongly in themselves and in each other. Back then, everyone had a super power. When we heard for the first time about the Darkness, it was when my great-great-grandfather was my age. People started losing their powers. Those who had been able to fly couldn't seem to do so anymore. At first they were still able to accomplish incredibly high leaps, but even these tapered away to nothing after a while. Those with the power of might gradually realized they could no longer lift even their own cars. All the power they had had begun to fade, and fear and doubt rushed in to fill the void. Eventually, when my great-grandfather was born, all super powers had disappeared from Encora. In only one generation, everything changed. And today, the majority of Encorians doesn't even believe in the prophecy anymore.

Eyes were still boring into me. "Yes, I do." I didn't know what they were going to do. "Punch me in my face or just say anything, but stop staring at me as if you want to kill me," I thought. Then, someone did say something. "Such a fool! Hahaha…!" He laughed straight in my face. And of course, everyone else did, too. It hurt more than a punch. I wished he had just punched me instead. I pushed my way past Mr Leather Jacket and his gang. I just wanted to go home.

I didn't cry but it hurt because they made me feel stupid. I felt miserable as I walked down the corridor. The same corridor I had so eagerly ran down earlier, on my way to my first Hero History class. Now, looking up, I saw the faces of our great heroes looking out from the paintings that adorned the walls. They were the first of their kind. When they needed to use their powers, they would transform. Only the very old ones could do so, and the feats they were capable of were astounding. One of them had a great power; he could turn into an immeasurably strong creature that could lift entire buildings from the path of danger. Another one was gifted with amazing intellectual prowess. He had designed and constructed a special suit that had enabled him to fly anywhere he chose.

Every single person in the past possessed exceptional abilities that made him or her extraordinary. And they embraced their own uniqueness. No one wanted to be like anyone else. Everyone loved who he or she was. I gazed at the parade of paintings, crestfallen. It took me a while before I finally stepped out of the building.

I didn't normally take this exit because all my previous lessons took place on the other side of the school. As I stepped out into the sunlight, I noticed that the ground was covered with patches of fallen leaves and a slight breeze blew. How quickly autumn came this year. I looked up at the giant sculpture of a boy taking centre place in the courtyard. I'd never had the chance to admire this magnificent statue before. He was holding a book in one hand and pointing into the sky with the other. The sculpture was massive. This gigantic boy had a mixture of excitement and curiosity on his face, the expression of an adventurer, someone who was going to change the world.

And right there at the base of the statue was the most beautiful girl I had ever seen. Sitting on the edge of the massive concrete base. She was writing in her journal, her hand moving fluidly, almost poetically, across the paper. Her expression was serious, yet a tiny smile curled the corners of her lips. She looked completely absorbed in her writing, journeying into realms unknown in her mind. She was an oasis of serenity against the backdrop of rustling leaves, chattering students and the majestic statue of the boy adventurer. It felt like she was channeling the energy of the world through her entire body to the tip of her pen. Gentleness and joy radiated from her.

I stood there for a few seconds, stunned, watching her. She looked up to the sky for a moment, tapping her pen softly against her lip, and then continued writing again, completely unaware that the brilliant colours of autumn faded in comparison to her quiet vibrancy. Silky shoulder-length black hair cascaded down her neck and covered the collar of the school uniform she was wearing. Her grey skirt blended in almost perfectly with the platform she was sitting on, enhancing the illusion that she herself was a sculpture, a thing of beauty forever captured in her stillness. I was transfixed.

I remember having already met her a few years back. That was the day grandpa brought me to the school for the first time. I'd seen this girl walking down the corridor as grandpa and I made our way to the principal's office. She had sensed my presence and paused, turning to look at me. Her gaze was at first inquisitive, but then it softened and she smiled at me, gently, probably sensing from my dazed expression that I needed all the kindness I could get that day. Grandpa frequently reminded me how dumbstruck I was after seeing her; I spent the rest of the day staring at the sky, thinking of the girl. But the memory felt unreal, blurry and distant, because that was the same day as my parents' funeral. Only two weeks before that, Darkness had killed my parents.

Insights:

Ask yourself three questions: Who or what does the gigantic boy represent in your life? When did you get knocked down because you stood up for something you believed in? Did your beliefs change after that, and how? Sometimes these three are interconnected. Perhaps, when you got knocked down, you stopped believing. And that belief that you let go of might be something as simple and as precious as "I am enough".

NOTES

Chapter Three: Death

Once everyone in Encora had lost their power, we needed to take drastic steps to keep ourselves safe, both from the Darkness and from the increasing amount of crime in the city. In the last few years, we had tried everything to protect ourselves from the Darkness. At first we thought we could just stay in the light, and we rigged up powerful lamps all around the city that could burn through the night, illuminating everything. But Darkness appeared all the same, engulfing everything even in places filled with light. We realized very quickly that just staying in light wasn't going to work for the long term. After that, we tried to build a defence wall. It was more than ten stories high and 12 feet thick. In our desperation, we even used nuclear weapons. The idea was that the blinding flash of light during nuclear detonation would kill the Darkness, but neither this nor the wall worked out.

The dome was our last chance. We had hoped that if we made the city completely impermeable, Darkness would not be able to enter. Encora, the last remaining city in the world, would be protected from the Darkness and the radioactive fallout from the nuclear detonation.

This dome now surrounded all of Encora. We were protected from the outside world, from ground to sky. The edges of the dome cut right into the earth and went several stories deep underground, so it was impossible for any creature to dig its way in, or for any radiation or Darkness to seep in. At least, that was the theory. Nothing and no one could enter or leave the dome without a permit, except for the guards and scouts, whom we deployed every now and then to look for signs of life or Darkness in our neighbouring abandoned cities.

Encora now looked like a gargantuan football stadium – a hundred times larger than your regular stadium. When we built that dome, we knew that there was nothing more we could do. Our last remaining hope was based on an idea of one of the professors from our school. He had invented a super shield, constructed out of a very expensive glass and diamond alloy, which we could use to protect the city from the nuclear radiation while simultaneously utilizing the sun's radiation to generate light – what the professor called an "Imitation Sun". This staggeringly immense shield was our dome. It absorbed the incoming radiation from the sun and projected it back. It was like a high-end reflector. It would certainly protect us from the nuclear radiation from our failed nuclear experiment. The professor, and all the people of Encora, hoped that it would also protect Encora from Darkness.

But even if it could keep out the radiation and Darkness, the dome couldn't prevent crime from happening within the city itself. People were starting to live in fear, now that they had no powers to defend themselves against Darkness and against crime. Crime was proliferating as people lost their regard for one another, so we needed guards to protect the innocent people from violence. Guards were the strongest, tallest and most dependable amongst us, and would risk their lives defending the city against any harm. If someone needed help, it was the guards' duty to step in and take care of them. Our guards were selected for their strength, loyalty, courage and concern for the people; not everyone could become a guard, and it was an honour to be one. But over time, this caring for someone else had simply become a job. It became rare to find guards who truly believed in honour, sacrifice and justice.

My parents, however, became such guards; in fact, they were amongst the best because they were really strong, tall and brave. Stronger than anyone else. When the Darkness came into being, my parents felt that they had to do something, and they wanted nothing more than to make the world a better place. For everyone in Encora, and especially for me. I knew they loved me. They always told me so. And that was why they did what they did.

It was a normal day. They were called to rescue a scout who got stuck in Phëalis, one of the abandoned cities a few miles away from Encora. When they tried to save the man, Darkness surprised them. They couldn't do anything. They couldn't run or fly away. It was too late. Once Darkness touched them, it was as if it sucked colour out of a painting. Life just left them. I was only six years old.

We didn't know much about Darkness at that time. We only knew it as a black cloud that appeared randomly. Sometimes it was just a small cloud that disappeared as quickly as it appeared. But mostly it appeared in simultaneous wisps, tufts, and patches, almost like a herd of sheep. And then it would silently grow. The mass of single clouds, steadily and stealthily increasing in number, would merge together into one big lethal cloud that engulfed everything in its path. Evil roiled in its murky depths, sometimes forming nightmarish shapes, sometimes looking inexplicably familiar to the people trapped in its deadly embrace. It never got tired. Its victims did.

And then: the touch. Guards described it as the silent finger of death. A quiet, surreal moment, a flash of resignation in the eyes and the instant collapse as life drained away. Some say the black cloud would grow faster when people were frightened, but it was hard to verify because people rarely escaped the Darkness alive. This was just one of the many myths about the Darkness.

My grandpa took care of me after my parents passed on. He loved to tell me stories about my parents, especially about the time they met each other in Guard Training class, in the very same school I was now attending. It was love at first sight, and from their teenage years, they knew they were going to spend the rest of their lives together. In the end, they had left this world together, too.

Each time grandpa talked about my parents, he added another detail. I didn't really know if the stories he told me were true, but that didn't matter. In that way, he made it easier for both of us to accept that they were gone. Sometimes it sounded like he was telling me stories about two superheroes instead, although my parents didn't possess any of the old super powers. Even though I missed them a lot, I wasn't angry that they couldn't be with me. They had died doing what they believed in, and protecting those who needed help. They were my heroes.

I reached home and went up to my room, still upset because of what had happened in class. At the same time, my mind was filled with thoughts of the girl sitting at the giant sculpture's feet. We'd never been in the same class, and the school was far too big to bump into her every day. But we lived in the same part of Encora. So I would sometimes see her passing by our house.

When I saw her today, sitting on the platform of the sculpture, I felt my heart skip a beat. I could not describe what it was, but it was certainly the best moment of the day.

She didn't notice me, and fortunately, I was conscious enough to not stumble and fall despite how captivated I was by her. I just walked silently past. It was something I was good at, having practised it almost every single day of my life. I was shy, and almost afraid of walking in the middle of paths, walkways, corridors or streets. People would stare at me. They would see that I was nothing special. They would notice. So I always chose to walk on the side.

"Are you there?" My grandpa asked. He was downstairs. I guess he was done with preparing dinner; delicious scents wafted through the house. Our agreement was that I cook on Sundays and he would do it on my school days. He didn't work anymore. He was once a school bus driver but he retired when I was in the seventh grade. He used to drive the bus that I took every day.

My grandma passed away many years ago, even before my parents. My mum had been only three years old. Darkness attacked more often back then, and sometimes whole cities got lost overnight. It wasn't easy for grandpa. He loved grandma so much and missed her terribly. Sometimes at night I would wake and hear grandpa crying. It must have been very painful for him. He has not only outlived his wife, but also his own daughter and son-in-law. Whenever I heard him, I would walk down the stairs. And without saying a word, I would climb up his comfy armchair and lean against his soft chest. He would hug me tightly, and sometimes I would feel his tear drops on my arm. His embrace would gradually loosen after a while, and I would feel his breath calming down and becoming gently regular. He would fall into heartbroken sleep that way, with his only surviving grandson comforting him.

Many people lost their loved ones. It was hard. Grandma had just been visiting a friend when Darkness overcame her, without sound or warning. Darkness was unpredictable, and no one could ever be sure which place or person would be consumed by it next. From that time till today, Darkness has been gradually, surreptitiously surrounding Encora. It was appearing more and more often and finally it didn't matter anymore in which direction we ran; Darkness was already there.

"Yes pop, I'll come down in a sec." I was looking at the picture I'd placed beside my bed. It showed me with my parents in the summer before the accident. I smiled. It was funny. My parents were tall and buff, while and I was skinny and not even half their height. Every shirt seemed ill-fitting on me, but I never cared because all that mattered back then was being able to hold my parents' hands and hear them talk about their adventures. Both of them were looking down at me affectionately, and I was smiling straight into the camera. A big smile with closed eyes and a gap between my front teeth. Two days before, I had just lost one of my front teeth. To me, it was the best picture I've ever had. On the back was written: "You are born for a reason. Do not ever doubt that." Instead of a signature my mum drew a little heart under the words. I touched the heart, imagining my mum drawing it while my dad looked on. I missed them. I still love them, wherever they are.

"The food is getting cold!"

"OK, I'm coming."

Insights:

There can be several reasons why we give up on our dreams or lose our self-worth. Most of the time, we all create a story which gives

us an excuse not to get back up on our feet and to do what we dream of. But even if we don't believe in ourselves anymore, there is always someone who believes in us. What is the picture or person you can go back to, to find what you might have lost?

NOTES

Chapter Four: The Letter

Green beans with rice and chicken. I loved green beans.

"Heavenly father. Thank you for the food, amen," grandpa prayed. "So boy. Did it work out? Did you change the class?", he asked while serving me the food.

"Yes, it worked out. Mr Braunsten signed the transfer papers so I could start the new class right away."

"That's good," he replied, piling beans on my plate.

"Grandpa," I asked without preamble, knowing he could almost read my mind after our years together. "How would someone know if he is the one the prophecy is talking about?"

The prophecy had been given by one of the most powerful amongst the old heroes. This hero had the power of clairvoyance – she could see into the future. Startling visions would appear to her, and they always came true. No one else has ever had this power after her. It was the time when Darkness first appeared. She foretold that one day, there would be a beloved son who was full of love and his love would defeat the Darkness. She could not see his face; his identity remained shrouded in mystery. But those who were present then witnessed a single tear running down her cheek as she saw, in her vision, the world enveloped in a blindingly beautiful light. But she also saw that until the beloved son appeared, within one generation, we would lose all our powers. At least this was what we learned in school, and also what my grandpa told me in his stories. Stories that his own grandpa told him.

He looked at me. "Seriously?"

"Yes. Because the prophecy doesn't mention that, does it?"

"Well. I think he or she will just know it by faith and I guess he or she will then naturally start to act differently."

I pondered for a while, wondering how one would know something by faith. We had been assigned some homework today, after the teacher had asked if we still believed in the prophecy. Perhaps there would be more clues in the homework.

"I think I should go do my homework for the Community class. They want us to read this letter and reflect on it," I said, after finishing my food.

"Yes. That might be a good idea," grandpa said while getting up to clean the kitchen. I took my plate and put it into the dishwasher. "Don't worry. I'll take care of this," he said, with a smile on his face.

"Thank you, grandpa."

I went upstairs into my room. My desk was in front of the window. From my chair I could see the giant glass dome which enclosed the whole city. It was the only thing keeping us safe from the encroaching Darkness. Sometimes the stars would shine through the dome, but not tonight. I wondered if we would one day see the Darkness pressing up against the other side of the glass, finding pinholes to slip through. I wondered if the dome would be enough protection. I wondered if we would ever be truly safe again.

Shaking my head to clear these thoughts, I took the letter out of my school bag and sat on my bed. *The Servant's*

Secret was written on the top of the letter. Many years ago, an unknown person had written it and addressed it to the citizens of Encora. A scout had discovered the letter, carefully preserved in an ornate tin box in an empty house, in one of the abandoned cities that had been scourged by the Darkness. So touched by the letter was he that the scout brought it back to Encora and presented it to our leaders. The letter was a window to our past, back when Darkness was at its peak and super powers had disappeared, but heroes like this writer still existed. Seeing the historical and moral value of the letter, our leaders decreed that it should be learnt in Hero History class. The letter also alluded to the prophecy, which was why my teacher had asked if we still believed in it.

"Well, let's get started," I said to myself, and I started to read.

"Dear Citizen,

Today is a very special day. It is my 85th birthday, and I've chosen not to leave my house even though they want us to move to Encora. This is why this letter is going to be my legacy. I was born in this place. And when the time comes, I will die in this very same place. For most of my life, I've known what a blessing it has been to grow up in this house. This is because I've had wonderful parents. The truth is that I have learnt everything about life and love from the beautiful example my parents have set. Words cannot express how thankful I am to have had both of them as my role models. I am still inspired by their wisdom and abundance of love, and dignified by the level of integrity and authenticity they have chosen for themselves, and empowered by how much love and trust they have created.

When I look at pictures of my siblings, I see men and women who courageously followed their dreams because they know that they have a huge amount of parental love, support and trust behind them. Because of this, they have left the nest with a strong belief in themselves and a steadfast love inside their hearts.

In one of his speeches, the mighty Chris said that we only know a good tree by its fruit. I have personally witnessed how my siblings have developed strong, lasting and supportive friendships and relationships. The amount of love they show to the people around them every day is astounding. But more importantly, they are a reflection of our parents. We are their fruit, and we only love like they did. They taught me that there is absolutely no shame in showing how much you love someone.

While Darkness started to rip our family apart, I constantly witnessed both of them demonstrating their affection to one another. They openly kissed and held each other in front of all of us, and even though sometimes it was admittedly rather uncomfortable, the fact that they have been so blatant about it has taught me that the people around me are too precious to not be reminded of how much I love and care about them every day. My parents taught me to recognise, affirm and honour the value of each and every person that has been put in my life. Whenever one of us didn't know what to do, my parents always helped us to become silent, so that we might hear how loud our heart is screaming and listen to the wisdom inside of it.

I wish that you would find a way to turn down all the noise, and that you start creating beautiful experiences as a friend, a human – be it man or woman, as well as a *great husband or wife. Be a great parent. I am so grateful to have lived a long life. It brings me to tears just thinking about the wonderful differences you are going to make to those around you by simply listening to your heart. You can be a difference to the person next to you; you can choose to love, to listen and to change yourself so you might make the difference this world is desperately waiting for. Just follow your heart, and it will lead you well.*

> *Until the beloved son rises,*
> *Your friend."*

Tears ran down my cheek. It was a beautiful letter. Who was this woman and why didn't she live with her husband?" I asked myself while looking at the letter. And that line, 'follow your heart and it will lead you well', was a phrase I'd heard since I was a baby. My grandpa said it ever so often – to my mum while she was growing up, to both mum and dad when they took on their duties as guards, and now… only to me.

My mind drifted away and I thought about my own parents and my grandma. So many of my family members had been killed by Darkness. I read the letter again and again and when I looked at the watch I realised that it was almost midnight. I had been sitting on my bed for quite a few hours. Time had flown by so fast while I was lost in thought. I changed and got ready to sleep. When I lay down in my bed, I was still thinking about the wonderful words of the letter. It had ignited a small fire in me, a fire that burned in remembrance of my own amazing parents. Before I closed my eyes, I looked outside the window once more at the roof of the giant dome. "How I wish things could be different," I thought, just before I fell into a deep slumber.

Insights:

When you think about your own future, or the future of your family or maybe even your country, one fact is inevitable: one day, you and everyone else around you will die. This might not be a nice fact to think about. But in order to create a legacy, we cannot afford to not think about it. Neither you nor I know the day we are going to die.

It is therefore important to ask ourselves: what do we want to leave behind when we depart from this life? It is not about how much time we have left, but rather how we spend the time we do have, that matters most. What is the need you want to address with your daily action?

"If you don't know your destination, how can you know if you are heading in the right direction?"

Write a letter about what you wish would be said at your funeral about the life you have lived. Then get more specific about the characteristics you need to have, in order to accomplish those things. And then start developing those characteristics from this moment onwards.

NOTES

Chapter Five: Laws & Fear

The alarm clock rang shrilly. Half awake, I rolled out of bed and trudged into the bathroom to get ready for school. After brushing my teeth, I jumped into my school uniform. I took my bag and went downstairs for breakfast. It was my usual routine, but something felt different today. Strange but not uncomfortable. I was tired as usual and the same annoying bird outside my window kept interrupting my favourite song playing on the radio. But somehow, while walking down the stairs, I felt... lighter. I was breathing somewhat deeper.

"Good morning grandpa," I said when I came down. He was already awake, having his coffee and reading the newspaper.

"Good morning. How was your sleep?"

"Actually I slept pretty good. What will you do while I'm at school today?"

"I might fix the garage door and get some groceries."

"Well. Please buy some green beans," I said, with the biggest smile I could manage so early in the morning.

"I will. Don't worry." He said, and took a sip of his coffee. I did the same. Then he looked at me, smiled and said, "You know my grandma once told me: Follow your heart and it will lead you well."

"Yes, I know. You've told me this I guess a hundred times," I said, while laughing. "Why are you telling me this right now?" I asked.

"I am probably going to paint it on the wall in our living room. What do you think?"

"Yes. That's a great idea."

With a smile in his face he returned to his papers. I finished breakfast and left for school, a skip in my step.

"Welcome to the Law class. Today, we are going to learn about the laws of Encora," our teacher said. There were some muffled groans from the students, followed by the listless turning of pages in textbooks. The Law textbook was thick. All of us had to memorise all the laws within.

School wasn't always like this. Back then, school was a place where people came together to discover their powers. To find out who they really were and then to learn how to use their powers to do good. Every single person and power was important. There was a culture of growth and experience at school. People knew that they could only find their powers in relation to other people. That's why we had only one school, where everyone could learn with and from each other. Yes, it was a big school. But no one had ever had difficulties finding their place. The school was a community. The students were a team, and the teachers their coaches. Trust, love and responsibility towards each other held the students and teachers together. They didn't separate us back then and there weren't so many rules.

Today we still have only one school, but now we mostly spend our time here learning about the past, memorising endless laws, revering old heroes and trying to decipher the Darkness. As I've said before, things have changed. Drastically.

"The first law is: You are not allowed to leave Encora. The second law is: Always stay inside the city." Those laws sounded the same to me. "You need to know," the teacher continued, "the law exists to protect us."

I was confused and said, "But isn't it that only people can protect people? How can a law protect us? It only shows us how helpless we are." My mouth was faster than my mind. Again every eye was fixed on me. Why couldn't I just be quiet?

"I'll talk to you after class, boy!" the teacher said to me, glowering. I shrank back in my chair and nodded miserably.

After the bell rang and everyone had left the classroom, he stood up and walked towards me. I didn't know what he was going to say.

"What's the problem?"

"There is none. I just said what I thought. I didn't mean to be rude, sir. I'm sorry." I really meant it, even though I didn't understand why no one else thought like me. It wasn't good to question the laws, I knew. Questioning the laws was tantamount to dismissing the safety of the people of Encora. No one questioned that which was put in place to protect the people.

"I don't want this to happen again. Am I clear?"

"Yes, sir."

"Then you can go."

Just another wonderful day in school. I could feel everyone looking at me as I walked towards the exit. Walking past all the pictures of the old heroes, I felt somehow like I didn't fit in anywhere, the way my shirt hung awkwardly off my shoulders in the picture with my parents. I stopped in front of one of the paintings. The hero depicted was one of our most legendary ones, named Chris. His power allowed him to manipulate matter and circumstances. He could change anything, actually. He could transform matter from one shape and state into another. He could even accelerate the healing process of diseases. The picture showed him giving a speech to a big crowd of people. At the corner of the picture was a written line from his speech, "…to seek the city of justice…"

"What's that… city of justice?" I asked myself while walking down the steps at the exit. "And what was this Chris talking about in his speech anyway?"

She wasn't there. The statue of the giant boy stood alone. "That's sad," I said to myself, shoulders sagging infinitesimally. I was hoping to see her there, to feel her calm, gentle, beautiful presence again. Instead, Mr Leather Jacket and his gang had taken over the platform at the base of the statue, lounging around and tossing their drink cans at each other. Maybe that's why she wasn't there.

I was so focused on what was in front of me that I didn't notice another student running towards me. He was facing the ground, face hidden within his hoody, so he didn't see me standing there. Inevitably, we clashed and both of us ended up lying on the ground, all his books were scattered on the stairs. It was that boy in my new class who seemed to avoid any eye contact. He looked around in panic, fearfully scrambling to get up on his feet, as if he wanted to escape. He immediately started picking up his books, dropping them as quickly as he could gather them in his skinny arms.

I bent down to help him, picking up the books that he kept dropping and trying my best to balance them in his trembling arms. While stacking the last of the books, I couldn't help but ask him, "Why are you so scared?"

"Darkness," he said, with an air of devastation. "How can you even ask this? I know you. You are the new boy in our class. You have no idea how it's like to be in this class. And anyway didn't you lose your parents? How can you not be afraid?"

I didn't really know what to say. His words hurt but at the same time I felt sorry for him. I noticed that everyone in my new class seemed to be perpetually scared, but for some reason, I wasn't. Each of my new classmates showed their fear differently, but it was obvious that they all lived in fear of the Darkness.

The boy mumbled a 'thank you' and disappeared into the school building before I could respond. I was so taken aback by my encounter with him that I hadn't even noticed Mr Leather Jacket and his gang leaving. I took the chance to have another look at the sculpture. I examined the face of the statue. This time, apart from excitement and curiosity, I saw one more thing. This boy's face was fearless.

"How was school?" Grandpa asked during dinner.

"I read something on a picture of one of the old heroes and I can't stop thinking about it."

"What was it?" he asked curiously. So I started to tell him what was written on the painting of Chris. "Maybe tomorrow you could go to the library where they have all the history documents. Probably you will find Chris's speech there."

He just smiled at me. That smile he had when he was up to something. I knew he could have told me much more about Chris, his speech and the Darkness, Encora and its dome. But for some reason, he wanted me to find out for myself.

Insights:
Sometimes a system can end up becoming a prison for our hearts. Many people live their lives not even knowing that they might not truly be free. Whenever we are part of a system like that, our natural instinct is to make sure the system isn't changed. As the saying goes, "If it ain't broken, why fix it?"

The truth is, a prison also works. Its effectiveness depends on it not being broken. But it keeps everyone in bondage.

It is important to know that people don't stick to a system or a prison with bad intentions. They just really believe that "it is the way it is". You just have to "follow the rules".

Have you ever felt, talked or behaved in a way that wasn't acceptable in the system you live in? Then I have a question for you: What was stronger than your need to fit into the system? What made you step outside of the system and free yourself? What specific need did you have or see? What did you feel? What made you stand up?

NOTES

Chapter Six: A Speech of Courage

"Good morning grandpa," I said when I came down for breakfast. As usual, he was already awake, having his coffee and reading the newspaper.

"Good morning, how was your sleep?"

"Actually I slept pretty well. Thank you." A day like any other.

Grandpa took a sip of his coffee and looked at me. "Don't stand there. It is already late. If you want to go to the library, you should leave soon. The library is only open in the morning."

"You all saw me perform such feats and I'm well-known to possess great power…"

I read the words of the mighty Chris voraciously while seated at a small desk on the third floor of the historic library of Encora. It was bright in here; the light made the place feel almost sterile. White, high walls full of books, white shelves everywhere and many groups of little desks spread all over the beige carpet. The library was a big white building in the middle of the city, right next to our school.

For the past two hours, I had been searching for the written speech of Chris. I finally found it. It was a really old speech, years before my time. My great-great-grandfather was probably around when this speech was delivered. Chris was a hero like no other. He went everywhere to teach about using the power for good. For a better future. In the year when Darkness appeared for the first time, he was well known. He gave his speech when all the citizens of Encora met in front of the town hall.

He hadn't come that day to teach and talk. Everyone was afraid because they saw or heard about our great heroes dying and disappearing while trying to defend humanity from Darkness. The terrified crowd called for Chris to save them, to comfort them, to offer his words of wisdom. So he stood up in front of all of them and started to speak.

"You all saw me perform such feats and I'm well-known to possess great power. But let me tell you something. You aren't going to believe this. But there will be a time we won't need these powers anymore. Because this time of fear and Darkness will pass and we will see the dawn of a better future.

Don't be afraid. We, as one people, will pursue a city of justice that will be brought about by the beloved one. We grew from not having any powers, to being blessed with all kinds of powers. The ability lies in us and it always has. It is not about power. It's about love. Love will be the birth of justice. The powers are gifts to help each other grow into our shared destiny. They are nothing but a tool to revive the dead part inside of us, the part that has stopped believing in love, in goodness and in ourselves. Our powers only serve to stimulate and inspire us to do good. So that we strive for a better tomorrow, a brighter future. What gives us hope is the greatest power of all – Love. Choose to love and you will be facing death. Choose to love further on and you will be love. There is no fear or Darkness in love. There is only love and light. And we will look to him, the beloved son of the prophecy. The one who will come to us, who will love, and even when facing death will never stop loving. He will love beyond death."

That was the most beautiful thing I'd ever read. I took a pen and carefully wrote, on my left arm:

"Choose to love and you will be facing death. Choose to love further on and you will be love. There is no fear or Darkness in love. There is only love and light. The ability lies in us and it always has been. It is not about powers. It's about love. Love will be the birth of justice."

These were the lines that resonated most with my soul. I drew a small heart under the words, like my mum did on the back of my picture. After that, I put away my pen, left the library and kept walking. My mind was blown by those few lines. I couldn't think or even concentrate on where I wanted to go. I just walked. I was lucky to finally turn onto my street. When I saw my house, it was as if the question I was searching for had finally found me. "If I could love this way, what would it look like?"

"You remind me a lot of your dad," my grandpa said. He stood in my room to wake me up for school.

"What?" I asked, groggily.

"He wrote things down on his arm and talked about love all the time."

'I guess he'd read what I'd written on my arm the other day,' I thought, while trying to rub the sleep from my eyes. Grandpa sat by my bedside and looked at me. I saw tears in his eyes as he moved his finger along the words on my arm. He was really touched by that line.

"I'm very proud of you. I want you to know that. And I think whatever others might say, your parents loved you so much that you are still whole. Your heart is not broken and therefore you are not afraid."

Grandpa's words washed over my heart and drove the last vestiges of sleep from my mind. I sat up in bed and we just looked at each other. My grandpa was wearing his black jogging pants and a white polo shirt. His eyes were framed by his glasses and his feet were neatly ensconced in his old sandals. He was my familiar, loving grandpa, yet at the same time I saw him with new eyes. He had just cried in front of me, and his words moved me beyond measure. I felt my own eyes fill up with tears. Slowly, I crawled over and hugged him.

"Thank you grandpa. I love you."

"Ok. You need to get ready for school," he said, while trying to hide how happy he was. We wiped our noses and I got up. "Breakfast is waiting for you downstairs," he said, while walking out of my room. I made my bed and put on my trousers. Only then did I realise that that annoying bird wasn't annoying me this morning. It wasn't even sitting at my window anymore. Instead, looking out of my window, there was only the small apple tree that my great-grandfather had planted many years ago, down in the garden. 'I should grab one of those apples for lunch today,' I thought.

Insights:
Stories are able to make us believe again. Movies, books, music or the arts in general can help us to reconnect with our heart. On the journey of rediscovering your dreams, be mindful of the movies you love or the

music you listen to. Sometimes these can help you get back on track and realign with what truly matters to you.

So what are your three favourite songs, movies, books, art, etc.? Why? What makes them special to you? What values do they represent?

NOTES

74

Chapter Seven: Decisions & Consequences

Darkness was the absolute absence of light. In the past years, guards tried many different ways to find out more about it. But they only lost more people. Until today, it is not clear where the Darkness came from, or how it came to be. It didn't seem to have been made by humans. It moved like a fog, but a fog with consciousness. It behaved like it knew who, what and where we were. It felt mindless yet sentient simultaneously. The only certainty we've had when it came to the Darkness was that it was relentless, and it killed everything in its path.

I mentally sieved through everything I knew about the Darkness as I left the house, hoping to find some more clues about the prophecy. Just as I turned to close the front door, I saw the girl again. She was in the backseat of her dad's car, and he was driving down the street I lived on. Time seemed to slow as my eyes widened.

Her family lived at the far end of my street. Even though we lived near each other, I rarely caught sight of her. Her parents were very protective of her, and she never left the house much. When she did, her dad would send her to her destination in his car. The destination was almost always school. On the rare occasion when I spotted her, either sitting at her desk at home, in her dad's car, or with her classmates in school, she always had a book or her journal with her. Her bright eyes sparkled whenever she was reading or writing; it was obvious that stories and words came alive in her mind.

At school, she was nearly always surrounded by friends. I had been lucky to spot her alone at the statue that day. People visibly brightened up around her, and she always had a ready smile for them.

I believed that she was always the first to sit with the younger new students, guiding them around the school campus or earnestly tutoring them. The younger kids adored her, and would gaze at her in rapt attention as she brought them through their homework.

Much like the way I was gazing at her now, as her dad's car drove past me and into the distance. So rarely did I manage to catch sight of her that today felt like an even happier one for me. It was enough for me, for now, just to see her. I never would have talked to her though. "What a wonderful day this will be," I said to myself as I strolled down the path towards the bus stop.

The school was only five stops from my house. There were buses going to every part of the city. Some parents chose to send their kids to school, but only a few parents had a car or even the time. Cars had become expensive ever since the traffic in the city became a problem. So they had to regulate the number of cars on the streets of Encora. Priority was given to our city's engineers, guards and leaders, as their duties required them to go around the city several times a day, sometimes at high speed.

Grandpa had the time, but as a bus driver, he didn't have a high enough income to own a car. So I was used to travelling by bus, although it hasn't been the same since my grandpa retired. When he was a bus driver, every bus ride felt like a stand-up comedy show. He was the funniest of all the bus drivers and everyone loved him. He made us forget about the world outside of the bus. He made the Darkness a distant memory. He brought smiles to the children. A bus ride with grandpa was a bus ride filled with happiness. He always said the smiles on the kids' faces were worth everything.

"What a wonderful day this will be." I thought about the girl while waiting at the bus stop. I looked at the group of kids around me. It was funny. At first glance, we all looked alike. Yes, of course it's the school uniform. But it also made me notice how different all our faces look. I wondered what stories these faces would tell me if I asked.

The bus arrived, on time as it always was. I leapt on board and strode to my usual seat. Ever since my grandpa retired, I would choose the same seat on the bus every morning. Not in the front, not in the back. Right next to the door, so I can get off the bus as soon it arrived at school. Bus rides lacked that excitement for me now that grandpa was not the driver, and I didn't want to stay on the bus any longer than I had to.

At the first of the five stops towards the school, Mr Leather Jacket boarded. He proceeded to walk towards the back of the bus but suddenly stopped next to me.

"I want to sit here. Move." He commanded.

Everyone in the bus was waiting for my reaction. I didn't say anything. Gripping the back of the seat hard, I looked at him as I stood up to change to another seat. He sneered as I left my original seat and started to laugh, calling me a fool. Then he got up and stood next to me again.

"I want to sit here, idiot. Move!"

A lot of things crossed my mind while I stood up to move to yet another seat. Mr Leather Jacket had a victorious smirk on his face as he watched me change seats. In a loud voice, he called me a wimp. Then he roared with laughter. Some other kids started to laugh as well. When the laughter had died down, Mr Leather Jacket stood up yet again, and again came to the place I chose to sit. I knew what was coming this time.

"Get up! This is where I want to sit!"

Decisions. We make them every day. A lot of them, in fact. But we rarely really consider our choices. We never truly think about what our decisions mean for our lives, or how they impact us. We choose in the present, but barely think about the cost for tomorrow.

When I was 5 years old, my parents got promoted to be the Guard Leaders. That was a huge honour and an even a bigger responsibility. They had three days to consider before making their decision. The first day, I remember that they were at home. Their leader had given them the day off. I remember it well, because it was the last day I saw them alive. We had spent the whole day together. We had breakfast, and then went back to bed. We watched a movie and afterwards we went out to enjoy the sun. It was summer and a refreshing breeze was blowing. We went down to the park and had a picnic with ice-cream from the ice-cream truck, and my dad taught me how to throw a baseball. With the index and middle fingers on the seams, so it wouldn't slip out of my hand. In the evening, they even read a bedtime story to me, both of them, together. It was the most beautiful day I've ever had with them.

They'd written me a letter which my grandpa had given to me on my 14th birthday. In the letter, my dad wrote:

"My beloved son, right now you are too young to understand, but you will when

you are older. We were asked to become Guard Leaders, and we know that this is our calling; it's our purpose, and we know it means we may lose everything. We know that if we choose to be leaders, we have to be prepared to give our lives and lead by example, and that will cost us everything. All our time, our energy, and even our lives, if need be.

Because you are either a leader, or you are not. There is no in between. You will come to understand, that you can't be a leader like you can be a taxi driver. It is not a job but a way of being. We will always be here, even though we are going to be busier than we were before. My beloved sun, one day you will understand that love is why we are here and love is why we will be free. We love you. I love you. Dad."

One day after he wrote this letter, they died. They would have become the official leaders the next day. They weren't the leaders yet, but they made a decision to lead by example, and when someone had to go out there to rescue a person in danger, they were the first two to stand up. They made decisions with full awareness of the consequences and the costs. They never backed down, they never gave in to fear, and they always made a stand for what was right.

Two weeks after my parents died, friends and colleagues from work came to my grandpa's place. It was the day of their funeral and I had just come back from my enrolment at the school. I had also just moved in with Grandpa, and I felt disoriented and overwhelmed. Everyone was wearing black suits, and they had brought food and flowers. I'd never seen so many people in our living room. There were so many people, even people I didn't know, who had come to pay their respects because they were so moved by my parents' sacrifice. Many cried and many made toasts to my parents. I listened to all the beautiful things they had to say about my mom and my dad, my heart full yet breaking at the same time.

While the speeches were still going on, I had gone upstairs into my new room. My stuff was still in boxes and the walls were blank and white, like a new life. When I sat down on my bed, I accidentally pushed one of the boxes. It fell and all its contents landed on the floor. I bent down, picked everything up and put them back into the box. Books, toy cars that my dad bought me, some pens. Then I picked up a white envelope, and I stopped. My name was written on it.

I slowly opened it and a small, folded piece of paper fell out. I picked it up and opened it. There it was, dad's necklace. It was made out of gold and had both their wedding rings on it. I looked at the rings. One of them was smaller than the other. It must have been my mum's. It was a bit thinner. But both the rings showed signs of years of work. Tiny scratches, not so shiny anymore. On my dad's ring, the engraving was only barely readable. And although the rings were so different, you could tell that they went through the so many experiences together. For years and years. "What a testimony of their love!" I thought.

Then someone knocked on the door. Shocked, I turned around. I held the necklace tightly in my closed hand and said, "yes?" It was my grandpa, and next to him was the girl I saw that morning in the school corridor. All the neighbours on our street had heard about the unfortunate passing of my parents, and about the poor little orphan boy. Her dad had been one of them, and he had come to offer whatever comfort he could to me and my grandpa. He'd brought his daughter, this beautiful girl, along.

I faintly registered her presence. I was lost in my own thoughts and heartache, focused only on what I had in my hand. My grandpa tried to talk to me but I couldn't hear him. I saw his lips moving.

"Hey boy, I'm asking you something."

I snapped awake from my daydream. "I asked you if you both would like to go outside and play for a while." He looked at me, then at the girl, and back at me again. He raised his eyebrow meaningfully at me, waiting for a reaction. Blankly, I looked at the girl. She simply smiled back. And my mental fog lifted.

"Yes, of course. Ok, come," I said. Grandpa gave me a worried look, not entirely sure that I was thinking clearly and hesitant to let me out to play with just the girl for company. But the girl, sensing this, placed a small hand on grandpa's arm and said, "Don't worry. I'll watch out for him." Grandpa seemed surprised; she was after all only six years old. Then he beamed, a sad but hopeful smile, and nodded at the girl. I was too dazed to be surprised. My hands still clutched my parents' rings.

We left the house and headed for the playground, which turned out to be between both our houses. It was the first time I'd been there as I'd just moved to this neighbourhood. We were silent the whole way, and I felt myself starting to panic, wondering if I should say anything to make things less awkward. But the girl merely smiled at me in understanding, a glint of mischief in her eyes, and shook her head. We didn't need to talk. I didn't need to pretend to be ok around her. She was here for me, and I didn't have to do anything to earn it. A small part of my mind, a part that wasn't drowning in grief for my parents, carefully stored the memory of that smile away. With one gesture, she did what no one else had been able to do since my parents died: she made me believe that everything would be ok again.

The only time we spoke that day was when she realized that I was holding something in my hand. As we crossed the street, I heard her voice for the first time. It was sweet and melodious, gentle and curious, yet confident and mature beyond her years.

"What is that in your hand?"

I stopped immediately. I'd been clutching the necklace and rings for so long that I'd forgotten they were still in my hand. Still in shock from grief and this surprisingly wonderful moment with the girl, I unwrapped my fingers. The engravings on my parents' rings had been imprinted on my palm because of how tightly I had been holding them. I held the necklace and rings up to her.

"Did these belong to your parents?" Such gentleness in her voice.

"Yes, it's my dad's necklace and both of their wedding rings." We stood in the middle of the street for a long moment, staring at the necklace and rings. She touched my palm where the imprints of the rings were and gave a sad little sigh. Then she smiled and asked me if I wanted to wear the necklace.

"Here, I'll help you to put it on. That way, you can keep them close. And you don't have to hurt your palm again."

"Uhm, yes, thank you," I stammered.

Another pertinent memory. A bittersweet one. Heavy grief meant that I stayed home for many months after that, unable to bring myself to play or experience joy while my parents remained dead. But gradually, the heartache healed. The wonderful memories of my parents smoothed out all the painful creases in my heart. But I never got to play with the girl at the playground again.

"Get up. This is where I want to sit."

I looked at Mr Leather Jacket, the memory of my last interaction with the girl still playing in my mind. Perhaps it was the gentleness and kindness of the memory that made me really look at Mr Leather Jacket properly, for the first time. His smile was cocky, and his lip curled menacingly, but deep in his eyes I saw a wavering flicker of dark fear. A fear that had been there for a long time. Suddenly it was clear to me. Mr Leather Jacket lived in fear that he tried desperately to mask with his bravado and bullying. Fear of rejection, fear of loss, fear of weakness, fear of the Darkness and death. He was suffering, his heart and mind strangled in the grip of a fear he did not know how to control, but he didn't dare to let anyone else see.

I felt my own fear melt away, and my heart softened. I felt a glow of compassion and love for him, this boy who really just wanted to be loved and to be told that everything would be alright. I knew he would rather die than accept that I'd seen through him, though.

Looking deep into Mr Leather Jacket's eyes, I smiled gently and said, "Ok, no problem." That was all. His grin faltered at my response, disconcerted by my gaze. He was speechless for a while, his defences crumbling. Just then, our bus pulled into our school. I smiled again at Mr Leather Jacket and stood up to alight with the rest of the students. Swallowing hard, he glared at me half-heartedly before hopping off the bus. He seemed subdued, somehow, like all the swagger and belligerence had left his body. I stepped off after him, feeling like a shackle had been lifted off my chest and replaced by a warm radiance.

The fearful boy who had collided into me the other day saw everything. He jumped off the bus after me, falling in step beside me as I walked to the school entrance. Right when we entered the school, he couldn't contain himself anymore.

"Why didn't you speak up or fight back? He was being such a bully!"

I smiled and said to him, "Fighting and harsh words can't change anything. But love and compassion can."

Insights:

The decisions you make have consequences that impact yours and other people's life, in both good and bad ways. Before deciding and reacting, have you looked deep beneath the surface to truly understand what drives you and other people?

Sometimes, you may choose to let your principles and your vision for yourself and others drive your thoughts, words and actions, instead of your emotions and pride. How do you feel about being dedicated to something more important than your own fear and ego? What is the beauty of being totally committed? How does commitment relate to trust?

NOTES

95

Chapter Eight: The Power of Words

These days, school was always the same. It wasn't so much about exploring; more about ignoring. Ignoring the fact that since the Darkness appeared, we haven't found a way to fight back. We just die. School became a place where young people were taught to fear, to run away and hide. And the system worked very well because fear became the common denominator. Every day, we covered a different subject. There is the Law, Science (which is about understanding Darkness), Our Community, Hero History and Guard Training (what was sometimes also known as sports). Our world became very small. About six million people in one city. That was all that was left. There were no global markets or intercontinental flights anymore. All of it got swallowed by the Darkness. We've lost so much.

From the roof of the school we could see the barely visible ventilation system of the dome, and the valleys beyond it. On nice days, during lunch break, I would go to the roof café to grab a coffee and sit down on one of the deck chairs, looking at the dome and wondering how life was like before Darkness, before the dome. The school was the biggest building in our city; you would need a guided tour just to cover the entire compound. But you didn't have to. Since everything changed, you just had one class in the same room every day. It had become rigid, mundane and boring. The students stopped flourishing because school wasn't an inspiring place to be in anymore.

Today's subject was Our Community. This subject was basically meant to train us to fear that outside of our community was death. Ok, to be fair, this is my opinion. Officially, it's about serving each other and learning how we can live together. But I've always doubted that. Today, for the first time since I read the speech from Chris, I had answers to the questions I always had. What is missing? Why does life look so empty? When will all of this be over?

In the last class today we formed a circle. The teacher wanted us to face each other while solving a problem. He explained: "Outside the city was a beautiful flower. The flower had the healing power to cure a child. The child was sick. The child was very young and would die without the healing flower. The parents of the child left the city against the rules to search for the flower. They were lucky and found it. They came back and their child was healed. The guards arrested the parents because they broke the law. Even though they said they did nothing wrong in saving their child. But to leave the city was against the law. Should they be arrested and the child given away to foster care? What do you think would be the right thing to do?"

Most of my classmates started to argue and to explain why the guards were right and the parents wrong. Others, however, said that it would be ok because the child survived. I was deep in my own thoughts while the argument went on around me. I guess I was the only one who didn't share the opinions of any of my classmates. The teacher noticed that I stood on neither side of the debate, and wanted to know what I thought.

"Thank you," he said, motioning for everyone to calm down and listen. "What do you think?" He looked at me, as did everyone else. Nobody said a word. It felt like the longest minute of my life. I took a deep breath.

"Neither option. It is true that the parents broke a law, and it's also true that the child was saved. But it isn't about being right or wrong, because we aren't meant to be perfect by ourselves. And if we are not perfect how can we be right or wrong? If we choose to see all of ourselves in the eye of eternity, without the fear of death, and if we could understand that none of us are perfect, what is missing then? Love is missing! It is all about love. Love makes the ultimate sacrifice. What will always choose the good of the other first? Love is the timeless beauty of serving because it doesn't seek itself and it doesn't expect anyone else to do the same."

No one, including myself, expected such an answer. The teacher seemed taken aback for a moment, but started nodding after a minute. He asked the class what they thought about my answer. But no one said anything. Surprisingly, there were no reactions. I expected that everyone would argue against me, or laugh, but they didn't. They just looked at me wordlessly, some in faint surprise, and some even in awe.

The school bell saved us. Without saying a word, everyone took their bags and left the room, until only I remained.

"Words," I thought, "they are so powerful."

From the moment I finished I hadn't moved an inch. I was frozen. My own words were like a sword, stabbing into my heart. After a while I couldn't hold them back anymore; the words fought their way through. It was almost like my heart needed to overcome my mind in order to find relief. My tears flowed. I couldn't stop crying. I sobbed so hard. It was as if I had finally found the explanation behind my parents' sacrifice. I felt like I had discovered a hidden truth inside my heart. My hands were wrapped around my head as my tears dripped down my face. My body sank lower and lower until finally I was kneeling on the floor. Relief, freedom, hope. I felt my heart beating strongly in my chest, and my lungs drew in fresh, clean air. I could breathe again. I felt like I had cast off my chrysalis, as if wings were unfolding from my back while my heart burst into joyous flame.

Insights:

What would you do in a conflict like this? What emotions did you experience when you thought about giving the child away? What thoughts ran through your mind when you thought about the importance of the law? What values are behind those emotions and thoughts? What values are behind you?

NOTES

Chapter Nine: Love & Light

A scream shattered my reverie. I had been crying freely, with wild abandon, for several minutes now. Startled, I lifted my face from my hands. I heard a shout. I looked up; the screaming seemed to be coming from outside the school. I heaved myself off the floor and strode over to the window. All I could make out was people running in all directions, scrambling frantically over obstacles, pushing each other aside and yelling hysterically.

"What on earth? What's going on?" I whispered to myself as the chaos grew outside the window. The scream seemed to come from close by. A second later, more screams followed. Many, many more screams. They were coming from just around the corner.

I grabbed my bag and dashed out of the classroom. My classmates were milling around the corridor, agitated and distraught, confused and fearful. They had heard the screams, too. When they saw me bursting out of the classroom and dashing down the corridor, they followed behind, a frenzied mass of panicking humans erupting from the exit of the school and pouring down the steps. They all fanned out, sprinting as fast as they could across the courtyard and the street and down the narrow alleyways at the start of the residential district. My heart was pounding faster and faster, thumping loudly and insistently in my chest. Adrenalin made my body shake. My eyes were wide, and perspiration started trickling down my neck, wetting my shirt. My mind was a hot, ringing flash of white, filled with the screams that I had heard.

I wasn't prepared for what was happening outside the school.

I seemed to be the only one left in the school compound; the only screams I could hear now seemed to come from outside. All the other students and teachers had fled; textbooks and stationery were strewn everywhere. Papers fluttered along the grass. The school campus looked like a ghost town. But my eyes were drawn to only one thing, lying still and silent at the bottom of the steps. It was the shy boy. The boy who was so afraid. The one who asked me why I didn't fight back.

He was lying there on the ground, dead.

Anguish filled my heart as my eyes widened in horror. I knelt down next to the boy. I couldn't understand what was happening, or why this boy was now lying dead in front of me.

The chilly autumn wind suddenly got stronger, blowing the last leaves off the trees. A cascade of orange brown leaves fluttered around me, coating the ground and covering the boy. Then, there was a sudden silence, like sound had been sucked out from the world, leaving a vacuum. My eardrums burned.

I lifted my head. That was when I saw it. Black, misty tendrils, creeping along the ground like fingers of smoke. The carpet of orange-brown leaves turned instantly grey as the dense curls of smoke touched it. It creeped its way along the ground, getting closer and closer to me. Finally, I had come face to face with the Darkness. Nothing could keep it out, not even our precious dome.

Gradually, I realised that the growing hissing sound that I was hearing was the sound of Darkness. It filled my ears like a pit of vipers. With it, all sound came imploding back into the world. The horrified screams of frightened people echoed through the streets. A car crashed into the platform of the giant sculpture I had so admired and burst into flames. I couldn't see anyone inside the car. Everyone everywhere was screaming and running. They tried to hide behind trees or underneath bigger cars parked along the street. Many of them ceased to move when the Darkness caught up.

Slowly, it dawned on me that this was the day we'd always hoped would never come. We thought we were safe. But we weren't. Everything that we had done was for nothing.

I started to run as fast as I could. Down the stairs, across the court, around the corner and across the street which led me onto Phëalis Avenue. After a couple of blocks, I dared to look back. What I saw chilled me to the bone. The misty tendrils I had seen earlier had coalesced into a gigantic black cloud which now loomed over the school. Darkness. Massive tentacles of black smoke emerged from it, slithering their way towards cars, houses and people. Several people had frozen in fright, and could only stare in mute horror as Darkness enveloped them in its deadly embrace.

"Why aren't they running?!" My mind screamed in frustration. My feet automatically chose a shortcut towards home as my gut instincts yelled at me to get home as fast as I could. As I bolted down the streets, I saw people everywhere, swarming over each other to escape Darkness. We were all like ants, frantically escaping from a fate of being boiled alive by molten lava. A family had just gotten into their car when Darkness materialised at their front porch, for just a second. I didn't stop to see what happened, but I heard the screams and saw the shaking of the vehicle. Then, the car stopped moving completely. All was deathly silent within.

The same thing was happening everywhere in Encora. When I looked up, I realised that the entire outside of the dome was now covered in a humongous, opaque, dark cloud. This Darkness seemed to have a malicious mind of its own, a mind that caused tentacles of evil blackness to erupt from it and penetrate the dome, permeating every corner. It was at this moment that I realised that the Darkness was conscious, and it was hell-bent on devouring everything. It had learnt to separate itself into different entities, sending parts of itself to wherever it chose – wherever there were screams and humans.

The Darkness was unpredictable. It could appear anywhere. In the backseat of the car, in the room next door, behind you or right in front of you. The playground, not far away from our school, normally full of children from the Kindergarten, was empty. Only the swing was moving, swaying eerily in the still air. On the ground in front of swing was a boy, motionless. He wasn't older than six. I could still see a slight shadow hovering over him.

I passed by my region's soccer field. Darkness had struck while today's game was on. It was quick and merciless. All the players were lying across the field, limbs flung in disarray, their skin a pale grey in colour. Most of the audience wasn't moving anymore. Only one girl could be seen tugging on the sleeve of her motionless mum, wailing in desperate horror. It was terrifying.

"Daddy, Daddy, Daddy!" A boy was screaming and holding his dad's hand. Both of them were running across the street, the dad dragging the boy along as fast as he could. The moment I spotted them, a car came careening out from the Darkness, weaving erratically and headed straight for them. The driver, unconscious or dead with his head on the steering wheel, couldn't stop the car. It missed the boy and his father by inches, swerved right and slammed straight into a petrol station. A huge fireball erupted almost instantly, and all the screams in the area were swallowed up in a big, fiery explosion. The whole place was burning. It was hell.

I found cover behind a big garbage container. I could see fire and fear in the eyes of the woman who was hiding under the car in front of me. The reflection in the woman's eyes showed me what was left of the burning petrol station, debris raining down around it. I was far enough that the explosion hadn't hurt me, but the concussive force of it had stunned me. I got back on my feet. Two more blocks and I would see my place. I ran, ignoring the screams around me. When I passed the playground near our house, I leapt to the right and ran along a little path between back yards. I arrived at the bus stop outside my house just as grandpa ran out, gasping for air, the picture of me and my parents clutched in his hands. I was about to dash toward my grandpa when a flash of blue caught my eye, and the world froze.

It was the girl. Her blue skirt was bright against the greying doom. She was standing in the middle of the street, staring defiantly at the growing cloud of darkness. She was only about fifty yards away from me, but it felt like a hundred miles. People where running every which way around us; it was complete chaos. The wind was picking up, and it howled and whipped around her, forcing people to grab on to buildings and cars as they ran, dragging themselves forward. In the midst of the commotion, another black cloud surreptitiously emerged from out of nowhere, directly behind the girl.

"RUN!" Mr Schmitt, who had just dashed out of his house, grabbed my arm and yelled, spittle flying out from his mouth. "RUN!" Darkness came bursting in through the dome in thick, squirming torrents, pouring down every street.

I stood there, captured by something way more intense than fear. "Beautiful" was the only word that came to mind, as I saw the girl in the eye of the storm, a frozen, fatal tableau of beauty and bravery. She refused to move, refused to back away from the

Darkness. Filled with the fear of death, Mr Schmitt let go of my arm and ran away.

The fear I had initially felt when I was running home from school was suddenly so small. Something else was growing in my heart, burning away the remnants of fear left. A sense of overwhelming peace came over me. I knew I didn't have to run. I just looked at her and started walking. Slowly, determinedly, my footsteps never wavering. Everyone else was running in the other direction, away from the threatening, growing cloud of Darkness that appeared behind the girl. The Darkness swelled and pulsed, growing so large that it covered the sun and cast a vast, cold shadow along the street. People around me tripped, stumbled and fell as they tried to escape the shadow. No one helped anyone else; it was every man for himself. Their eyes met mine. Helpless eyes. Fearful eyes. Eyes that asked me, "what are you doing?" and, "where are you going?" It was utter, hopeless pandemonium.

I took one step after another towards the girl. I felt this warm tugging in my chest that pulled me towards her, towards that massive deadly cloud. I couldn't and didn't want to ignore it. The closer I got to her, the stronger and warmer the pull became. My chest swelled and I felt my muscles tighten beneath my shirt as the pulling sensation got stronger. I was standing only a few steps in front of her now. My chest almost hurt.

She still hadn't moved whatsoever. Still staring into the Darkness, her eyes had progressively lost their focus, mesmerised by the swirls in the evil depths of the black cloud. Her look was now empty. But somehow, a part of her still found the strength to stand tall and firm against the rushing wind and the energy-sapping fog.

Although I was staring straight into her eyes, she didn't seem to notice me.

The warmth from my chest was now climbing up my throat like it wanted to reach her. But no words came out. It felt like the warmth recognised her as a part of me. I reached out my hand to her... just as Darkness touched her back. A silent scream poured from my mouth. She collapsed on the ground.

Never before had I seen Darkness so close. I could have touched it with my fingertips. I could have coiled its tendrils around my finger. So, that is what my parents saw before they died. This evil, turbulent mass that sucked you dry. This finger of death. I looked down at the girl, the warmth from my chest now a blazing heat.

The screaming around me had ceased. The people in my street had stopped running. I couldn't see them as they were behind me, but the screams had suddenly faded away and I could sense their curious, terrified eyes burning into my back. I could see grandpa out the corner of my eye, still as a statue, watching me to see what I would do. For some reason, it felt like grandpa was smiling. I didn't turn to look, though. My eyes were fixed on the girl.

There she was, lying in front of me. Time seemed to be standing still now. As still as her heart. She was dead. I could feel it. The burning heat in my chest started to hurt. The searing pain made me bend over. "What is happening to me?" I asked myself. The slow-moving fog consumed more and more of her lifeless body. I was paralysed by pain, numbed by this awful sadness in the pit of my stomach. I could only see her arm on the ground now. The only part of her not yet engulfed by the fog. The rest of her was gone.

I looked at my outstretched hand, still reaching towards the girl. What was that on my left arm? Perplexed, I squinted hard at the blue smudges on my skin. The scorching pain in my chest abruptly vanished when I realised what the smudges were. It was the quote I had written down, from the speech by the great hero, Chris. As I read it, over and over, the blistering pain in my chest was replaced by a powerful warmth. I felt strength flowing from my heart, down the lengths of my arms, to my fingers. I felt the heat spread throughout my entire body. Over and over, I read the words out loud. Suddenly everything made sense.

"Choose to love and you will face death. Choose to love further, and you will be love. There is no fear or Darkness in love. There is only love and light." Further, I read, *"The ability lies in us and it always has. It is not about strength; it's about love. Love will be the birth of justice."*

I grabbed the necklace around my neck, the one with my parents' wedding rings hanging from it. The necklace that the girl had put around my neck on the saddest day of my life – a day that she had somehow managed to fill with a little bit of her light. The courage flowing from the rings filled my palm, my arm, my shoulder, my chest and streamed through the rest of my body. The pain was obliterated. I stood up straight and took one step forward into the fog. Into death.

Slowly I opened my eyes. I could see. It was not dark. I saw her body lying on the ground, still lifeless but as beautiful as always. Her face was peaceful. I looked behind me, out of the churning mist, and noticed that some people had started running again. Several others just stood there in shock, staring at where I had walked into the fog. The fog had parted, then closed behind me, like a curtain. You couldn't look in from the outside. I saw blurred movements and heard muffled screams. In the distance, I saw my Grandpa. He hadn't gone anywhere. Even though I was certain that he couldn't see me through the fog, I had this unshakeable sense that he was somehow still watching me.

I looked down again. Kneeling next to her, I took her hand and held it gently in mine. I could feel the warmth from my chest and palm flow into her. I could see the colour slowly returning to her cheeks.

"Come on, get up," I whispered softly.

She took a deep breath and opened her eyes. Her fingers gripped mine.

"I will not let you go. Never. Don't be afraid, there is no reason to be. Darkness is just a place where we haven't chosen to love yet." I pulled her to her feet. For a moment we just stood there, looking into each other's eyes. The fog around us became more turbulent, and distant screams were still filling the air. One small tear ran down her cheek. Her eyes had that calmness in them. I knew her. My heart knew hers. She leaned forward and hugged me. I suddenly noticed how the tendrils of Darkness couldn't quite touch us anymore. As if held at bay by an invisible force field around us, forming an expanding, protective bubble.

And in that moment I felt that warmth in my chest getting stronger again. It filled up my whole body, and hers too, streaming from my fingers to hers and pouring through her entire body. Both our chests began to glow, brighter and brighter, in time with our heartbeats. Beams of bright, golden light shot out from us in all directions, erasing Darkness wherever it hit. The light was pulsating, every pulse brighter and more powerful than the one before.

With every pulse, the light reached further through the city. The screams of terror faded and were replaced by sighs of relief, laughter and cheers. And I felt her throughout, in sync with me. I knew her, I recognised her soul. It was us who had defeated Darkness. It was love. I felt a hand touching my shoulder. It was Grandpa. As I turned around, I wrapped my arms around him.

"You knew all …" – "Shush." He interrupted me. "Yes, I did. And I will tell you as I told your father when he was a boy: "My *beloved son, one day you will understand that love is why we are here, and love is why we will be free.*"

- The End -

NOTES

124

NOTES

125

A Note from the Author

Let me tell you something about myself...

I finished school when I was 15. My teachers never really got my attention, which didn't help me to be a good student. "You study for life, not for school." You hear that, but sometimes you still don't feel inclined to study. I definitely didn't. Back then, I wasn't the smartest kid and I also wasn't really ambitious, even though I had dreams. I saw myself somewhere else. Not that I didn't appreciate what I had, but when my teacher asked us in 4th grade what we wanted to be in future, my answer was different from my classmates'. I said, "I want to become a president." Yes, I was always quite confident. My classmates reacted as if I had stood up and started to give a speech along the lines of "I have a dream, that one day..."

Today, I know that primary school is the time when your childhood dreams are still alive. When "being realistic" hasn't had a chance to kill them yet. A boy wants to become a fireman, a police officer, an astronaut, a fighter or a cowboy, or a part of the Avengers or one of the Guardians of the Galaxy – simply, a hero in his own way. Because we sense somewhere deep inside of us that we are important, and our lives should be meaningful ones. What I know now is that sometimes your heart can show you something about yourself that your mind would never dare to dream of.

As I've said, I never really studied, and it took me until I reached the age of 21 to realise that I also never worked on my dreams either. I had so many dreams and ideas but I never did anything about them. I did not understand that a dream remains a dream until you translate it into action. Someone asked me once, "If you could live your life again, do you believe you could do more then you have?" My answer was a resounding "Yes". And in my case that is true. What influenced my actions back then was my belief system. When I was 16, I wrote my first short story. But it took me another 11 years to start believing that I could be a writer.

We are the product of our habits and what we tell ourselves over the years. I told myself I couldn't be a writer because my German grammar was poor and I completely failed in English. The only thing I knew I had was imagination. But imagination doesn't count if I don't do anything about it. That's why I got bad grades and I chose not to learn English at all, until I met someone very special. It's not that I didn't like to learn the language; I just believed I did not have what it took to learn it.

"Someone's opinion about you does not have to become your reality!" When I heard that sentence for the first time, I cried. That sentence has stuck with me ever since. I believed so much in the negativity that other people saw, and never thought to trust in the good things about me that they didn't, or couldn't, or wouldn't see. And so, I let their opinions as well as my bad grades become my reality. It's like this: If you grew up in a family where people went through heart-breaking experiences, you will probably hear: "Don't trust easily." You've got a high chance of having trust issues. And what happens to love if we don't trust? At times, I still fight with my victim mind-set. And sometimes, it really knocks me down. But I want you to know: You are enough. You have more than what it takes to get back up on your feet. And more than that: you are loved.

Closing Words

There are tons of things worth sharing at the end of this book, but there is only one moment I think, which is significant for me. The one moment in my life which literally changed everything and simultaneously inspired me to write the Fading Darkness story.

Sometimes it goes back to a single event. When you choose to believe in something greater than yourself. For me, it was in the year 2013, the 30th of March, at lunchtime. I was in the UK attending a conference when a friend of mine said "I want you to meet a friend. She is a dancer and wants to open her own studio, like you did." Everyone back then thought I had opened a dance studio, but to be honest I merely had wonderful friends who did. I was just the guy who was lucky to be their friend.

A few moments later I found myself shaking hands with this random and completely amazing girl. This is the moment I'm talking about. It was magic and I still don't understand it, especially for me. I've always believed in love, but lately, I was breaking hearts and disappointing people more often than not. I didn't stop believing in love though; I just thought maybe this kind of love wouldn't find me. "Hello, I'm Sebastian it is nice to meet you," really, I said it as kindly as I could. She was really attractive, and I would have held onto her hand forever it hadn't been completely strange to do that. So I just shook her hand like a normal person would. But truth be told, I was stunned like never before.

"Nice meeting you too," she said. To me it sounded like she was speaking with the tongues of angels. The same ones that announced the birth of baby Jesus. That was the moment that literally changed my life.

Sounds dramatic, and yes, it was. This is the significant moment I was talking about.

Have you ever had a moment you thought you had been waiting for your whole life? This was mine. My moment of truth. My personal love story moment. If you know his books or the movies, this was my "Nicholas Sparks" moment. A fairy-tale moment, when a prophecy is spoken out loud. You never can extinguish it again. It is spoken. Like a seed, which starts growing until the young man comes and pulls Excalibur out from the stone. I didn't know exactly what it was, but I felt something so strong.

The girl and I chatted late into the night, and when I went to bed I said to my brother, who was sharing a room with me. "She is the one!" I was never so convinced about something in my life before. I say this because I've never felt like this before, and simultaneously, I'd lost all logic. At that point in time, I could hardly communicate in English and she didn't speak German, and as if this wasn't enough, our relationship started as long-distance one, which means we only had language to build up our future. Life is such an ironic friend.

I didn't know what I was going to go through, but sometimes, everything starts with believing in something bigger than yourself.

A random day, two random people but that was the moment when I chose to believe in the light within me.

About the Author

Sebastian Schick is a Personal Development Coach and Leadership Trainer in the field of experiential training and performance coaching. Originally from Germany, Sebastian now resides in his lovely tropical island home of Singapore with the love of his life.

Prior to his career in the personal development arena, Sebastian was a renowned professional dancer and choreographer, co-creating one of the most successful ballet and breakdance crossover productions in Germany.

Sebastian is passionate about people, leadership and love. He believes that in life, everything is possible – the impossible just takes a little longer.

Fading Darkness – Turn On the Light Within You is Sebastian's first book.

Connect with the author, Sebastian Schick, at www.sebastianschick.com.